TOTALLY WORTH CHRISTMAS

A Copper Country Novella

MARA JACOBS

Copper Country Press, LLC

Published by **Copper Country Press LLC**

Copyright 2013 **Mara Jacobs**

For more information on the author and her works,

please see http://www.marajacobs.com/

ISBN: 978-1-940993-84-3

Prologue

❦

The Friday night after Thanksgiving

I still say we need to go to a strip club," said Charlie Simpson's best friend, Jeff.

Or, at least he *used* to be Charlie's best buddy. Charlie wasn't so sure anymore.

"I don't think so," Charlie said. For about the sixth time that night.

These days, he only saw Jeff when he made it home to Port Huron for the holidays or some other event. And that was fine with Charlie.

"Come on, man. You've been a total pussy all night. If that's the case, I say we go look at some real pussy."

Jesus, Charlie thought.

"Jesus," somebody said quietly. Charlie looked across the booth at his other two pals, Ricky and John, but it hadn't come from them. Apparently they didn't hear it. Then Charlie saw the waitress walking away from the booth next to them, coffee pot in hand. It must have come from her.

He took a closer look at the retreating figure. Figure being the key word. It was hard to gauge her age from the back, but if the white-blond ponytail swinging across her shoulder blades was any indication, she wasn't as old as the gray-haired waitress who had been waiting on Charlie's table. This woman was petite, but with lots of curves. Curves that swayed and glided under the retro, knee-length, polyester diner uniform the waitresses wore at this throw-back joint.

Tiny and curvy. A million miles away from the tall and lean figure of Deni Casparich, the woman he worked with and, up until last February, had considered his soul mate.

Well, okay, maybe not soul mate. If he was being honest —and Deni living with their boss, Sawyer Beck, had forced honesty upon Charlie—maybe less soul mate and more best friend who was conveniently of the opposite sex and also conveniently as single as Charlie.

"I'm serious. Let's go find some fun. Enough of your emo bullshit," Jeff said, pushing at Charlie to exit the booth. "You get home, like, twice a year these days, and I'm not going to let you piss and moan about a chick for the entire time."

"I've said maybe two things about Deni this whole night," Charlie said as he cleared out of the booth, then stood aside so Jeff could exit. John and Ricky did the same, both reaching into their wallets and putting some bills on the table. Charlie did as well.

"Yeah, you may have only mentioned her twice, but it's obvious that's where your head is at. Both of them," Jeff said with a stupid chuckle. Charlie noticed that Jeff hadn't reached into his own wallet. Charlie put a few more bills on the table.

"So?" Jeff said to them all as they stared putting on their coats. "Pussy Palace? Or do we take the bridge to Canada?"

John and Ricky both opted for staying in Michigan, and Charlie tried to figure out how to gracefully get out of going to a strip club with his buddies. All he really wanted to do was go home, maybe heat up some of the turkey left over from his mother's Thanksgiving dinner, and then hit the hay.

He lived and worked in the Upper Peninsula, an eight-hour drive from Port Huron. He had come home on Wednesday after work and was heading back Sunday. He used to spend these short visits partying with his friends, but if his attitude tonight was any indication, he'd be spending Saturday night home with his parents watching something on Netflix. And he looked forward to it.

As he reached for his coat on the hook beside the booth, he noticed the small, curvy waitress talking with their older waitress behind the counter. She still had her back to Charlie, but he made out what seemed to be the older one handing off her tables to the younger one. She was untying and removing the pink apron from the front of her uniform and handing over her order pad to the younger woman. The older woman pointed at Charlie's table, and the younger woman looked over her shoulder to them.

And right at Charlie. Bam.

"Umm…you guys go ahead. You're right, Jeff, I'm in a pissy mood tonight. I'd just be a drag at the club. I'm going to finish my coffee and head home." He took a quick look at his coffee cup, praying there was some left. Not that he wasn't going to totally ask the waitress for more the second his buddies were out the door.

He let his coat stay on the hook and slid back into the booth, like he'd only gotten up to let Jeff out. Like he'd intended to stay.

And not as though the bolt from seeing the waitress' face, coupled with that body, wasn't what made him sit his ass down. No need to draw anybody else's attention to her.

Luckily, she now followed the older waitress through the doors to the kitchen, and Charlie inwardly sighed with relief that none of his buddies had seen what a looker had been just yards away from them. No way would they be heading off to a sleazy strip club when they could watch this woman walk away from them for a couple more hours.

Ricky and John seemed undecided, hovering between Jeff, who was already zipping up his coat while shooting Charlie a dirty look, and Charlie sitting back in the booth.

"Seriously," Charlie said to them. "Go ahead. Have fun. Place your dollar bills strategically. Give me a full report tomorrow."

That seemed to be all Ricky and John needed, following Jeff out of the diner, with only a "Later, dude," trailing behind them.

The people at the table next to him cleared out, and there was only one other booth on Charlie's side of the diner with customers. He couldn't see around the corner of the L-shaped counter to know if there were other people still left or not. He sipped from his coffee cup, taking only the smallest amount, willing the cute waitress to come out from behind the swinging kitchen doors and notice him.

As if the gods had heard him, the door swung in Charlie's direction. He held his breath, praying it was the young waitress. It was. And she was heading in his direction. But then she stopped when she saw him sitting in the booth. She turned around and headed away from him, and Charlie almost screamed in frustration. But no, she was only going to the coffee maker and grabbing a pot of the blessed brew and bringing it…yes, she was…bringing it to him.

"Care for a refill?" she asked as she reached him.

"Hmm-mmm," he mumbled, holding his cup out to her. God, had the words "care for a refill" ever sounded so sexy? Her voice was light, airy and had a familiarity to it that went right to his gut. Up close she was even more angelic looking. Her face was heart-shaped, and her eyes were a deep brown that seemed a stark contrast to her light blond hair.

"There you go," she said, filling his cup. She turned to walk away, to leave him, and he blurted out, "I didn't go with them."

She turned back to face him. "Excuse me?"

He put his cup on the table and motioned to the empty seats in his booth. "My friends. I didn't go with them."

"Oh-kaaay," she said in a be-nice-to-the-mental-patient kind of way.

"I know you heard them talking about going to a strip club."

She shrugged noncommittally, and he wondered if maybe she hadn't caught as much of their conversation as he thought. And, more importantly, why did he care one way or another?

But he did. Suddenly it seemed so....

"Important," he said. "It's important to me that you know I didn't go with them."

"Listen, it's none of my business if you—"

"But I didn't. Not that I haven't ever gone to one. And I might have even gone tonight, just…because… But then I saw you."

"Me?"

"Yes. I saw you, and it was much more important that I stay right here and hope you walked by than to go out with my buddies."

The coffee pot in her hand dipped a couple of inches, but she didn't drop it. She did, however, take a much closer look at Charlie. Her scrutiny should have made him squirm, but he held her gaze, didn't look away.

"You would have had better luck at the strip club," she finally said, then turned and walked away. When she reached the counter, she put the coffee pot back on the burner and went through the swinging doors.

What the hell had he just done? Totally uncool. She was probably hustling out the back door. Or getting a big, beefy short-order cook to come out and kick Charlie's ass.

The door swung again and Charlie braced his hands on the edge of the table, fearing the worst. But no burly cook came out with the waitress. She was alone, carrying a tray. She made her way over to the only other table with diners —a couple in their twenties who sat on the same side of the booth together. She took the bill and cash that they held out to her, and she said something Charlie didn't hear. She made her way over to him as the couple left the booth, put on their jackets, and left the diner.

Leaving Charlie alone with his dream girl. And potentially a kitchen full of people.

She made her way to Charlie, putting the money the couple had left her in her apron pocket, still balancing the smallish tray on the open palm of her right hand.

"Hey, I didn't mean to freak you out or anything," he said to her as she stopped in front of him. "I just…." He couldn't finish. She'd turned those rich brown eyes on him, and he lost all thought.

"You didn't freak me out," she said, as she pulled a plate from her tray and set it in front of him.

He stared down at the plate, which was covered with a very generous helping of pie.

"Banana cream," she said. "Gladdie makes the most amazing banana cream pie you've ever tasted."

He took his eyes from the enormous confection and looked up at her. She was so close to him that if he moved his elbow, it would graze her nicely curved hip. Much as he wanted to, he didn't move his elbow, but instead picked up his fork and took a bite of pie.

Rich, creamy, and yet light-as-air taste exploded in his mouth. "Oh my God," he said, his mouth still full.

A bright smile crossed her face. It was sweeter than the pie. "I know, right? To die for isn't it?"

He nodded, stunned by her thousand-watt smile. She left him again, but this time she didn't return to the kitchen, but instead locked the front door, turning the "open" sign around. Then she flipped a switch, turning the outside sign light off.

"Are you closing?" he said.

Idiot. Of course she was closing. "I mean, do you need me—" he started.

She held up a hand as she walked to the wall at the far side of the room and turned off some of the lights. Most of them, really, except for the one nearest Charlie and the ones over the counter.

"You're fine. I've got lots more to do yet. It's my night to do all the post-close stuff. Enjoy your pie."

He enjoyed the view more. Watching her turn off things, and cleaning others. Charlie had never eaten more slowly in his life. His forkfuls barely held any of the voluminous pie, trying to make it last as long as possible, while she finished the business of closing up.

Finally, he'd finished the pie and it seemed she'd finished her tasks. She made her way over to his booth. "So, was the pie better than going to a strip club?"

"Definitely," he said, smiling at her, waving at his empty plate. "Thanks."

"No problem," she said. He expected her to walk away, or hand him his coat, but she just stood there, watching him.

"You're probably in a rush to get out of here, to get home." He tried to put some questioning in his voice, and tried not to look too pathetic... or too hopeful.

She shrugged, leaning her hip against the back of the booth facing him. "Umm, well, I have finished up all the stuff I'm supposed to..." He sat quietly, not moving a muscle, hoping there was a "but" at the end of that trail off. "But," (*Thank you, God!*) "there are always more things that can be done."

"Before you start those, do you want to sit down?

Would you like to talk a little? I'm Charlie, by the way." He looked at her nametag pinned above the pocket on her uniform. "Phee," he said.

Phee. Short for Fiona? Not that it mattered to him; he liked the sound "Phee" made as it rolled off his tongue.

She looked closely at him. Charlie tried to look as harmless as possible. *Just someone to share a cup of coffee with at the end of a long day. Certainly not some guy who believes you just may be the cutest thing he's ever seen.*

She took a deep breath and let it out, like she'd just made a big decision. To Charlie it felt like it may very well be one of life's turning points, but he didn't want to put that pressure on her.

She slid into the seat across from him and said, "Yes, I'd like that." She smiled brightly at him and then put her head down as if shy. "I think I'd really like that," she said so quietly Charlie almost didn't hear her.

But he did.

And he knew that somehow his life had totally changed in this retro diner, nearing midnight, as he sat alone with a waitress.

Chapter One

❦

Three weeks later

Y ou lifted your head. Try it again," Darío Luna said to Charlie, then tossed him another golf ball, which Charlie teed up on the driving range mat.

"It didn't feel like I lifted my head," Charlie said, but he took his stance again, determined to keep his eyes on the ball.

"Dude, you're really gonna argue with a two-time Masters champion?" Petey Ryan said from his chair where he sat and watched Charlie hit.

Charlie's head came up, and he looked at Darío. "That's not what I meant. I hope you don't think—"

Darío held up a hand. "Not at all. I know sometimes it feels as if you don't move, but your head does come up just before you make contact."

"Because I really do appreciate you taking the time." It

was true. Not many people got a professional golfer giving them pointers. And all for the cost of a beer after they were done.

"And we appreciate all that you did for us in making this place a reality," Darío said, his arms encompassing the huge indoor driving range that Charlie's employer, Summers and Beck, had designed.

The driving range had been open for just over four months and was seeing a nice steady flow of traffic. Considering that the first snow had come to the Copper Country in mid-October this year, it would be a long winter. Having this outlet for the local golfers who would have months and months before they could get back on the course was a nice benefit for the community.

The place was empty now, though, with just Charlie, Darío, and Petey in the cavernous, dome-shaped structure. It was ten at night, an hour after closing, though Petey had been talking to Darío about keeping later hours as the winter progressed.

Charlie took another swing, trying to concentrate on keeping his head down through his entire motion. The club made a crack against the ball, but not the pure, solid crack that came from Darío's swing. Charlie looked down the range and saw his ball skittering along the turf, like a stone skipping across a still pond. Not exactly the effect he was going for.

"Worm burner," Petey commented from his chair.

"Yeah, I got that," Charlie shot back.

"Don't get your panties in a wad," Petey said. "I was just trying to help." The giant of a man had an angelic look on his face that made Charlie crack up.

"Big help. I can see it was a shitty shot, thanks."

Petey flashed a grin and leaned back in the office chair he'd wheeled out from behind the counter once the place had cleared out and it was just the three men.

"What's up with you, anyway? You usually like my commentary."

That was true. Charlie had grown to like Petey's rude comments and crude jokes when they'd worked together on the driving range project. It had been a group effort, but Charlie, not wanting to spend much time with a newly-in-love Deni and Sawyer, worked as closely as he could with Petey and Darío. Somehow that had morphed into Darío giving Charlie some pointers on his swing.

What passed for a swing, anyway. He took another whack at the ball and at least this shot got in the air before hitting the ground. Fifty yards down the range.

"You'll be totally fine, as long as every hole is only seventy-five yards long," Petey said, chuckling.

Charlie saw Darío shoot Petey a warning look at which Petey shrugged.

A few shots more and Charlie packed it in for the night. "Can I buy you guys a beer?" he asked both men.

Darío shook his head. "No, thanks. I want to get home and see if Katie needs any help packing."

"Why are you packing so soon? You don't leave for Spain for another three weeks," Petey said.

"We think we'll go to Florida first. Katie's parents are down there for the winter now, and we thought we'd bring Peaches to them, seeing as it is her first Christmas."

"Like when? When would you leave?" Petey asked, coming out of his chair and approaching Darío.

"We're going to drive this time, take our time. We're planning on leaving Thursday. " Which was three days from now.

"No. No way," Petey said. "You can't leave until Sunday at the earliest."

Charlie wasn't sure what kind of agreement Petey and Darío had come to about the staffing and management of the driving range, but he thought Petey was handling all of that now that he was living in the Copper Country full time. From what Charlie had seen, Darío seemed more of a silent partner who stayed out of the day-to-day operations and only used the range for his own practicing when in town and it was too cold to go to a real golf course.

"Why does it matter if we wait until Sunday?" Darío asked. "Is there some reason I need to be here for the driving range?" Apparently Darío had the same impression Charlie had of Darío's responsibilities to the joint venture.

Petey waved a huge hand of dismissal. "Range, schmange. I've got this thing running like a well-oiled machine." Charlie and Darío looked around the structure. Petey had done a great job with the place so far. And it seemed to Charlie as though Petey really enjoyed the time he spent working on growing the business.

"You'll miss our party if you leave on Thursday," Petey said. A tiny bit of hurt was in his voice.

Charlie had a flash of the invitation to Petey and Alison's holiday party that was sitting on his own desk. "Oh yeah, that's right. I meant to tell you I wouldn't be making it." He couldn't really remember if he was supposed to RSVP or not. The invitation had arrived the day after Charlie had gotten back to the Copper Country from his trip to Port Huron for Thanksgiving. He'd been in a shitty mood all the way back and the following day at work. When he saw the invitation to what would be a fun party, but full of couples in love, he'd thrown the damn thing on his desk where it still sat.

He didn't have other plans for Saturday night, but he knew he did not want to be anywhere near the joviality that would come from a Petey-hosted party.

"No. No, no, hell no," Petey said. He pointed a finger, first at Darío and then at Charlie. "You are both coming to our party on Saturday." His finger moved back to the Spaniard. "You. You'll head to Florida on Sunday." Back to Charlie. "And you. You will put on a suit and tie and show up at my place. I don't care what kind of funk you've been in for the past few weeks. You will be gracious and kind to Alison, and have fun, goddamn it."

"It's just that I—" Charlie's words died as Petey shot him a look that no doubt had had NHL players quaking in their skates.

"Zip it. This is Alison's chance to show off the house. The house that she has—*thank you, Jesus*—chosen to share with yours truly. She's really happy with how the renovations went and she wants to share *our* home with all *our* friends for a little holiday cheer." Darío started to open his mouth when Petey added, while looking at Darío, "And if it would make *your* woman happy to have her house full of her friends, then don't tell me that you wouldn't make it happen."

Darío closed his mouth. "*Sí*, I would." He sighed. "We will leave on Sunday."

"Thank you," Petey said, then turned his stare to Charlie.

"I barely know Alison," Charlie said.

"You grew on her. And you drew up the changes to the house for us. She wants you there," Petey said, shrugging, like if that was what Alison wanted, who was he to question it.

And apparently Charlie wasn't one to question it, either.

He could launch into how being around couples having fun would sting like a son of a bitch right now, but then he'd have to talk about that night, and he wasn't prepared to do that yet. Even to these two men whom he'd grown fairly close to over the past eight months.

It was still too raw, too fresh. It wouldn't help to relay the good parts—they played over in his mind constantly. But so did the day after, when he'd gone back to the diner to see the woman he knew was going to be someone significant in his life, only to find her gone, with no word on how to find her.

He'd felt like a dupe, a total idiot. The feeling hadn't gone away on the eight-hour drive back to Houghton. And hadn't lessened much in the ensuing weeks.

Petey moving toward him pulled Charlie out of his maudlin memories. Before the hulk could take another step closer, Charlie put up his hands in surrender. "Okay, okay. I'll be there. Do I need to RSVP or anything? I can't remember."

"Consider yourself accounted for," Petey said, then turned around and started wheeling the chair back to behind the counter. "Bring a date if you want," he added, though he didn't turn around.

Good thing, because Charlie couldn't cover the twinge of pain that rushed through him, knowing the only woman he would want as his date to Petey and Alison's party was hundreds of miles away and hadn't wanted to see Charlie ever again.

Chapter Two

"Here Gran, let me help you," Phoebe Robbins said, leaping up from the couch to help her grandmother Clea, as she entered the room.

Her grandmother waved her off, but Phoebe hovered over the older woman until she reached the couch and settled on it. "I just had to get out of that bedroom. I was going stir crazy."

"You're doing so great, Gran. Who would know you had a stroke just a few weeks ago?"

"Mini-stroke," Gran corrected her. "Not much more than a fainting spell, really."

"Hardly," Phoebe said, but she knew better than to argue with her grandmother. The woman was tough as nails, and Phoebe had assumed Gran would outlive both Phoebe and her older brother, Finn. So, when she got the call on a Saturday morning a few weeks ago that Clea had suffered a minor stroke, Phoebe had been shaken to the core.

And then she'd packed her bags.

Clea and Finn had raised Phoebe, giving up a lot to make sure Phoebe was taken care of. She knew they'd shielded her from her alcoholic mother's neglect. There was no way she wasn't going to come back and help with Clea's recovery, even though Finn had told her she didn't need to.

But she *did* need to. She needed to repay all that Gran had done for her. And Finn too, for that matter. Finn, who had two great kids from his wreck of a first marriage and baby Sam with his wife of almost two years, Lizzie.

Who was now coming in the door of the trailer after a quick knock. "Hi, guys, just thought I'd— Clea, you're up! *Should* you be up?" Phoebe's sister-in-law Lizzie asked as she entered the room, making sure to stand on the entry rug. Even the short walk from Finn and Lizzie's farmhouse across the yard to the trailer had put a packing of snow around Lizzie's Uggs. As Gran answered Lizzie with her stock "I'm fine, fine," Phoebe watched a chunk of snow fall from Lizzie's boot onto the entryway rug, a puddle already forming. It reminded Phoebe of that magical night such a short time ago, and a pang of regret went through her.

She shook her head, as if to shake away the memories that had haunted her nights these past weeks. And her days. And, well, hell, just about any time she was conscious. Wait, she dreamt about that night with Charlie, too, so technically all the damn time.

"You *are* looking good," Lizzie was saying to Gran as she kicked her boots off and took off her coat, draping it over a kitchen chair. She made her way into the living room to join Phoebe and Gran. "Which makes me feel better about stealing your companion for the night."

Huh? Phoebe looked at Lizzie. "Me? Steal me? What for?"

"I need a date for my friend's party tonight. And you, my dear sister, need a night out."

"What about Finn?"

Lizzie rolled her eyes. "You know your brother. He hates stuff like this. And I have to go, they're my best friends. And I *want* to go. It'll be fun. Alison hasn't let us in the house since they started the renovations. This is the big reveal. When I mentioned to Finn that you could go in his place, he jumped at the chance. He's getting some of Sam's stuff together and then they'll be over to stay with Clea until we get home."

Being around Lizzie's friends, people she'd met briefly at the wedding and Sam's first birthday party a couple of months ago, didn't sound like a great night out to Phoebe. But then sitting home and thinking about Charlie and that perfect night didn't seem like such a great idea, either.

"I don't have anything to wear. I think I have some heels, but I didn't bring any dresses or anything."

Lizzie was already nodding. "I thought of that, and I have a plan. I assumed you wouldn't have packed your party clothes when we called about Clea. You're just about Alison's size, so I called her and asked if she had anything you could borrow."

Phoebe had met Alison twice. She did seem about the same size, but still. "I barely know the woman. And it's her party. I'm not going to just barge in and rummage through her closets."

"No, of course not. We're going to get there early. She

needs a hand with some of the set up anyway. We can do that and then find you something to wear."

Phoebe was getting to know her sister-in-law better in the past three weeks since they'd been in such close proximity helping with Gran. She narrowed her eyes at Lizzie. "Is this just some elaborate plan so you get to be the first to see Alison's house?"

Lizzie waved her hand as if Phoebe were crazy, but there was a small flush of red on Lizzie's cheeks that seemed to be more from embarrassment than the walk over from the house. "Of course not. This is the best plan. Finn gets to stay home, and you get a night out. Win-win."

"I don't know…."

"I think you should go, honey," Gran said. "You've been stuck here with me ever since I came home from the hospital."

"And I've loved every minute of it," Phoebe said honestly. Her grandmother had needed minimal care, and a nurse had come to look in on them the first few days after Gran had been discharged. After that, Phoebe had been more of a waitress than a nurse. And she knew how to waitress.

She'd also loved reconnecting with her grandmother on an adult level, having left the Copper Country when she'd turned eighteen. Sure, she'd been home for holidays here and there, and Stevie's and Annie's—Finn's older kids—occasional birthdays, but for the most part, she'd been a child when she'd last spent this amount of time with Gran.

And yet, part of her still felt like a child, wanting to put her head in her grandmother's lap and cry over a boy, like she used to in middle school.

"Yeah, maybe it would be good to go out," she said to Lizzie, who clapped in delight.

Finn entered the trailer then, fourteen-month-old Sam in his arms. When Sam saw his mommy clapping, a big smile crossed his face, and he started clapping, too.

"That's right, big guy, give the ladies a hand," Finn said as he dropped a diaper bag from his shoulder on the same chair onto which Lizzie had dumped her coat.

Sam stuck a mitten-clad hand in front of him. "Hand," he said, proud of himself, looking around for praise.

"Yes it is, my bright boy. Very good," Lizzie said and rose to take Sam from Finn's arms. Phoebe's brother took off his own coat and then proceeded to peel Sam's jacket from the wriggling boy as Lizzie held him.

When Finn had Sam's coat and mittens off, Sam reached one hand to Lizzie's cheek and said, "Mama," with boisterous good cheer. Lizzie smiled and nodded, turning her head to kiss Sam's hand. The little boy then reached out with his other hand and placed it on Finn's chest. "Da."

"Yes, Sam. I'm your Da," Finn said. He looked past his son, who had a hand on both Finn and Lizzie, to his wife. The look of intimacy that ran between them made Phoebe look away. It was good to see her brother so happy. He'd had a lot of hard years due to his first wife and Annie's health issues. There wasn't a man in the world who deserved a break more than Finn.

And Lizzie had been his break. And his love.

Phoebe again thought of the night with Charlie—of the intimacy that had erupted so quickly and yet so naturally between them. For a moment that night, she had thought she'd met *her* break.

And then the phone had rung early Saturday morning with Finn calling about Clea, and Phoebe had packed up her car, paid her roommate for the rest of the rent, called the diner to quit without giving notice and hit the road.

No way to find Charlie—completely her own doing. Damn it.

She sighed and rose from the couch. Lizzie put Sam on the ground and the little guy wobbled his way the three steps to Phoebe's legs, which he grasped for leverage and then hugged. "BeeBee," he said with glee.

"BeeBee can't play with you right now, Sammy," Phoebe said, bending down to rub his little back. Such a sweet thing. "BeeBee has to get beautiful," she added, rolling her eyes at Lizzie. She then led Sam to Gran and made her way to the back of the trailer to get what little she had to party prep with.

"Yay," Lizzie said. She turned to Finn and said, "You're off the hook. Phoebe will go with me."

"Well, yeah, I figured. That was your plan, after all." He reached for his wife, who went willingly into his arms. Phoebe watched from the doorway to her bedroom as her brother hugged his wife and whispered something into her ear. Lizzie swatted at Finn's arms, but returned his grin.

"It'll be late," Lizzie said, pulling away from Finn, though not very hard. Finn pulled her back to him and kissed her soundly. "Wake me," he said to her with a very purposeful look and released Lizzie, who was smiling.

Phoebe turned and entered her room. Determined to go to the party and have a good time, she looked around to see what might be salvageable for a night out within her accessories and shoes. She'd have to hope something in

Alison's closet would work for her. Because seeing Finn and how much he loved his wife just brought back pangs of how much she'd like that in her own life—someone special, someone to connect with.

She'd thought that maybe she'd found it.

But no.

Chapter Three

✿

Y ou know you didn't have to come home, Phoebe.
We would have looked after Clea," Lizzie said as
they drove to her friend Alison's house.

"I know. But she did so much for me—so did Finn. It's
time to come home and help. Besides, I wasn't leaving much
behind." Which was true. Her life hadn't exactly worked out
like she'd hoped.

After graduating from Houghton, she'd wanted to get
out of Finn's hair. Finn, who by that time already had Stevie
and an AWOL alcoholic wife.

College hadn't been an option, for both academic and
monetary reasons. So, she'd moved to Flint first, and then
Detroit, and had started waitressing. Once she'd turned
twenty-one, she'd got on as a cocktail waitress at one of the
casinos. It'd been good money for someone without any
college education. She'd roomed with a couple of other girls
that she worked with. They'd done the clubs and party scene
in their early twenties. But then the Detroit economy

tanked, and she'd been laid off. She moved to Port Huron with her then-boyfriend.

One of many loser boyfriends to whom she gave more of herself than she ever came close to getting in return. They'd broken up six months later, but by that time she liked Port Huron well enough to stay. So, she'd moved in with yet another roommate, waitressing at the diner she'd left in the lurch when she'd come back to the Copper Country a few weeks ago.

"Well, it's been great having you home, really getting to know you. I know Clea, Finn and the kids have loved it, too."

"Me too," she answered. It was true. It'd been great spending so much time with family. Reconnecting with Stevie and Annie, her nephew and niece. Stevie hadn't started school and Annie hadn't even been born when Phoebe had left for down state. Now Stevie was sixteen, Annie was an active twelve, and baby Sam stole Phoebe's heart on a daily basis.

"So, the 'not leaving much behind' statement? Are you considering moving back permanently? It would be so great." Lizzie voiced the sentiment Phoebe had been feeling of late.

"I'm thinking about it," she said. Lizzie gave a little squeak of approval. "Don't tell Finn. I'm not sure yet, and I don't want him nosing in. I'm almost thirty. I can make these decisions myself."

"Of course you can. Finn knows that." At Phoebe's snort of disbelief, Lizzie added, "He does. Truly. It's just he'll always be protective of you, Phoebe. He'll always want what's best for you. But ultimately he just wants you to be happy. If that's in Port Huron, he can live with that."

"I wasn't all that happy," Phoebe said with more sadness in her voice than she had realized she felt.

The car was silent for a bit as Lizzie drove them out of Houghton toward the road that ran along the canal where Alison and Petey Ryan had renovated his waterfront house. To make it their home. Apparently they'd been living together since last winter in Alison's cute little cottage on the other side of town, heading toward Chassell. Phoebe had spent a day there last summer with Lizzie, Finn, and the kids.

"Did Alison sell her house?" she asked, suddenly interested.

Lizzie shook her head, not taking her eyes from the snowy road. "No. Not yet, anyway. She's debating whether to try to sell or just hang onto it for a while. They just moved into Petey's place a week ago. He'd been renting his place out when he was gone for the season. When they decided not to rent it this year and that they'd live there instead of her place, they took the opportunity to make some changes to it." A smile lit across her face. "I secretly think they were turning it from a bachelor man-palace into something more kid friendly."

"Oh, do they have kids?" Phoebe didn't remember hearing about that, or about them getting married, but she didn't really keep tabs on the goings on in the Copper Country.

"No, not yet. Not even married or engaged, though Petey told me he's asked a bunch of times. But I have a feeling they might be announcing that Al's pregnant tonight."

"Really?"

Lizzie shrugged, her wool coat bunching at the shoulders. "I don't know. She's been really jumpy about this party. That they're even *having* this party doesn't seem like them. They're pretty low-key." She smiled again, and her voice had a sing-song quality as she said, "I just think there might be some baby news tonight, that's all."

❧

If Alison was pregnant, she sure wasn't showing, Phoebe thought, as she and Lizzie were greeted by the hostess upon arriving.

"Come in, come in. Thanks so much for coming early to help. They just delivered all the food and it's in the kitchen. I'm having everybody just put their boots and stuff in there," Alison said, pointing to a large room off the garage entry that doubled as a laundry/coat room. "I need to figure out where everything will go once the party starts, but I need to keep some things in the oven, and...." She looked around distractedly while Lizzie and Phoebe took off their coats and boots.

"It's okay, Al," Lizzie said in a soothing voice, putting her arm around her friend. "We'll come up with a plan. It'll be easy. Besides, it's just close friends, right? That's what you said?" Alison nodded. "Then nobody's going to care about stuff like that. You know us."

Alison nodded again, then let out a large sigh, visibly relaxing into Lizzie's hold around her. "You're right, Lizard."

She took another deep breath and let it out. "It's just a party of friends. So what that we've got pretty dresses on instead of swimsuits and cut-offs. These are my peeps."

"Exactly," Lizzie said, squeezing petite Alison's shoulder. "And only one of us has on their pretty dress, so we'd better get moving."

Lizzie's dress was indeed pretty. A shiny blue wrap dress that accented her tall, curvy body and made her black hair stand out. It wasn't any wonder that Finn wanted her to wake him when she got home.

Alison was in yoga pants and a sweater and Phoebe wore jeans and a sweatshirt, though they'd both done their hair and makeup already. Phoebe carried two pairs of heels, one black and one red, not knowing what dress choices she'd find.

"The red. Definitely," Alison said to her, leading them to the kitchen. "I put a few choices in the guest room closet. Feel free to go on up. Petey's out getting more ice, so you won't bump into him."

The kitchen looked like a tornado had hit. Dishes sat on the counters. Trays of food, some wrapped in foil, some in Saran wrap, were all over the table and every other spare space. At one end of the table, it looked like Alison had dumped all her silverware and linens.

"Um, yeah. I can choose and dress quickly. Why don't I stay down here and help you guys first?" Phoebe said.

Lizzie was already diving in, moving things from here to there, organizing. "Yeah, let's get this stuff sorted so I can see what all you did—Oh, my God, these countertops are gorgeous."

Lizzie oohed and ahhed over the differences in the

remodeled kitchen. Having never been there before, Phoebe just saw it as a beautiful kitchen in a huge house.

Phoebe could appreciate a house like this, but she didn't need it. She'd be happy with just a home of her own. And a decent man to share it with.

She made herself busy at the end of the table organizing and setting up the silverware. When she got to the cloth napkins, she sat down and started folding them into an intricate design. She ran her hand over the completed ones, and a small smile crept across her face as she remembered the last time she'd folded napkins in such a way.

Chapter Four

The Friday night after Thanksgiving

P hoebe set the plastic busing tub full of clean linen napkins down on the table and scooted back into the booth across from Charlie. The only blinds she'd left open were the ones at the booth behind him, and from where she sat, Phoebe could see the snow was falling in large, fluffy flakes. Buddy, the cook, had left an hour ago with her assurance that she was fine, Charlie was harmless, and she'd be perfectly safe in the closed diner with a man she'd just met.

Buddy had seemed skeptical, but had grudgingly left through the back after coming out front and giving Charlie the once-over. "Boy wouldn't hurt a fly," he'd said to Phoebe as he passed her on his way to the kitchen and the back door.

Phoebe agreed. Charlie seemed like the stereotypical boy next door. Sweet, nice, safe. And yet, when he'd said he'd stuck around because of her, the heat in his eyes had been anything but safe. That heat had made Phoebe bring him the pie and ask him to stay. The sweet, nice, safe, was what had her telling Buddy to go and leave them alone.

"Go on," she said to Charlie now. "We were on this Deni girl whom you never made a move on." She took one of the napkins from the bin and began folding it into an intricate design. They'd talked about all of their past romances. Phoebe wasn't really sure how they even got on the topic. Something about why Charlie's pals had wanted to cheer him up with a trip to a strip club.

Charlie waved a hand, then grabbed one of the napkins from the bin and tried to mimic her actions. "No, I think we were still on Carson."

"Ugh. Please, no. What an idiot. Of course, I was the idiot who followed him, so I guess we were a good match."

"But he got you to Port Huron, which got you to this diner." He stopped folding and looked from her fingers to her eyes. "Which got us to tonight." He held her gaze and she couldn't help but smile at him. It was crazy, but she felt the same way. Not an immediate connection, because she'd thought he was just part of a group of yahoos stopping in between parties. But as soon as he'd spoken to her, she'd felt…*something*.

Which of course she didn't trust, her judgment in men not being the best. But on some level, she'd known those guys from her past were no good for her, even though she'd forged ahead into disastrous relationships. And on some level, she knew Charlie was different.

What she was feeling as she sat across from him— keeping her hands busy with the napkins so she didn't leap across the table and run her fingers through his adorable, tousled, brown hair—was different. He was wearing a white, thermal long-sleeved tee that reminded her of home, and a comfy, navy sweater that made his eyes seem almost blue, though Phoebe thought they were probably more of a gray.

She guessed him to be about her age, though when he'd tried to do the last name, where ya from, how old are you, what do you do for a living thing, she'd stopped him cold. That's how she'd gotten into trouble with men in the past—knowing everything about them. And yet, knowing nothing *real* about them until it was too late. If she only had this one night with Charlie—and he did get out that he was in town visiting his parents before she'd stopped him—then she wanted to know the *real* Charlie. And so they had talked about past loves, future dreams, words spilling out of both of them, a kind of giddiness at diving into real stuff and not just talking about what high school they went to.

"Yes. He got us to tonight. So, thank you Carson, wherever you are, you total dirt bag." They both laughed. She liked his laugh, kind of throaty and yet natural, like he laughed a lot. "So," she said, returning to folding napkins, though she'd have liked to stare at him longer because he was just so cute. "Back to Deni. You were crazy about her and never made a move. Why?"

He fumbled with the napkin, still trying to create just one, while she'd done several. She slowed down her movements so he could follow. "I don't know," he said. "At first, after she got together with Sawyer—that's the guy she's with—I thought I'd blown it by not making a move sooner. By being her friend and secretly, silently, hoping for more.

But now…" His fingers tangled with the napkin and he squashed the cloth in his hands. "Unbelievable. I'm an engineer. I design whole buildings. Why can't I fold this scrap of material into a stupid flower?"

She laughed and put her completed linen rose into the bin, then took the napkin he'd been working on. She smoothed it out flat in the space on the table directly between them. "Look, it's not that hard," she said, taking his hands in hers. She laced her ring finger and pinkie with his on each hand, keeping their thumbs, pointer and middle fingers free. Slowly, she began the folds that her grandmother had taught her years ago, Charlie's fingers working in tandem with hers. When Gran had taught her using this same method, Phoebe hadn't been breathless like she was now, her hands entwined with Charlie's, feeling the strength and heat in his movements.

They completed the flower and Charlie pushed it toward the bin, but continued to hold onto her hands, now lacing all their fingers together, their wrists resting on the table. His thumbs began to caress her palms, and she rested her elbows on the table, moving forward in her seat. Wanting to be closer to him, to feel more. His thumbs continued on, sliding back and forth across the pads of hers, then back to her palms, lightly following her life and love lines. Lines she just somehow knew this man would become a part of.

"But now," he continued. Phoebe had to clear her head to remember where they'd been in the conversation. Oh, right, that girl he liked. "Now I think that I didn't make a move on Deni for a reason. That I knew she wasn't the one. That I love her, yes, but like a buddy, a dear, dear friend."

Phoebe closed her eyes, letting his soft voice and softer touch melt over her, like the hot butterscotch she drizzled on the famed sundaes she served at the diner. "Because, when I saw her with Sawyer—how she looked at him—I knew that wasn't how I felt about her. And I knew...I just knew...I'd look at somebody someday the way she looked at him."

He tugged on her hands, and she opened her eyes. "And, Phee?" he said, a questioning tone in his voice, almost a confusion of sorts.

"Yes?" she said, her voice catching. She knew what he was going to say before he said it. Knew, because she was thinking the same thought.

"It's the way I'm looking at you," he whispered.

"I know," she whispered back, as if the feeling, the emotion, was too fragile to speak too loudly, lest it be frightened away. "Me too."

Chapter Five

❦

Three weeks later

Charlie ran his finger along the folded napkins on Petey's kitchen table. He'd never seen a napkin rose in his life, and now he'd seen one twice in a matter of weeks.

Damn, could he not shake the memory of her? It was driving him nuts.

He'd made the rounds of people in the living room when he'd first arrived; most he knew through Petey and Darío, or from having lived and worked in the Copper Country since he came to Tech at eighteen. It was a small party, an intimate group, and Charlie felt a little like the odd man out, knowing the hosting couple for probably the least amount of time. And of course, being single. So, he'd made his way to the kitchen, the one that he'd designed for Petey and Alison.

Designing kitchens—hell, designing houses—was something he hadn't done since his first year with Summers and Beck. He, and the company, had grown into much larger projects. But he'd enjoyed doing the house plans for Petey.

He looked around the state-of-the-art room. It was cluttered up with stuff for the party, but it was still a gorgeous kitchen. He liked it. And Petey had told him that he and Alison spent an inordinate amount of time in the room in the short time since they'd moved in. Of course, Petey had said it with such a grin and drawl that Charlie imagined they weren't doing much cooking. Especially since Petey had made it a point to tell Charlie there had to be room for a long, large, very sturdy table.

Moving away from said table, Charlie grabbed himself a beer from the washtub full of ice and bottles of beer and wine that sat in the sink. He leaned against the counter and slowly sipped from his bottle, looking around the room. He added the room to his never-ending list of rooms he would design for himself when he finally got around to building a place of his own.

He'd rented since he'd moved here, but had always planned to build. He'd just never gotten around to it. But now…he was ready. He wanted a home of his own. He wanted what all the couples at the party had.

But he wanted them with a woman he couldn't find.

"I can just dump out the beer, fill it with water and drink from that. No one will be the wiser," Katie Luna was quietly saying as she made her way through the swinging kitchen door, her husband Darío behind her. (Petey had also demanded a door be put in the kitchen instead of the open floor plan so many people desired these days. Charlie could only imagine what went on in this room that they didn't want seen through the wall of windows in the great room.)

Katie's look of dismay upon seeing Charlie in the room made him mentally backtrack and dissect what she'd been saying as she'd walked in. Darío, behind her, looked guilty. Charlie replayed her words in his head, but still wasn't getting it. Probably a chick thing.

"So, you have heard about our secret," Darío said. As the door swung closed behind him, he made his way toward Charlie and took two beers from the tub.

"Umm..." Charlie said, not sure what was going on, but guessing he should have figured it out. But his mind had been thinking about all that Petey and Alison were probably doing in this kitchen, which had morphed into what Charlie had done recently up against a different sink.... "I'm not...ummm...."

"It's just that we're not ready to tell people yet," Katie said, walking over and taking one of the bottles from Darío and emptying it in the sink. "I mean, there's no reason not to, I suppose. It's just that...well, we're so stunned ourselves. Peaches isn't even a year old yet. We certainly weren't trying. I mean, we weren't *not* trying, but, well, you know..." She rinsed the empty beer bottle out a few times and then proceeded to fill it with water. "And I always drink beer. Lizzie and Al know I'm not nursing anymore, so they'll figure it out." She reached out with her free hand and linked it through her husband's arm. "I don't know. Maybe we should just tell them?" she said to Darío.

"Oh, you're pregnant," Charlie said, finally getting it. The couple looked at him like he was the dunce he probably was.

"*Sí*. We just found out yesterday. And we were a bit… shocked, to put it mildly," Darío said.

"Wow, you're going to have your hands full," he said, then wished he hadn't.

Katie's breathtakingly beautiful face squished up, and a few tears pooled in her eyes. "Oh, my God, I hadn't even thought of that. There's no way we'll be able to travel with you now. It was hard enough with one baby, but with two?"

Darío put his arm around his wife and pulled her close to him. Katie buried her head into his shoulder. "We'll figure it out, *Gata*. I don't have to travel as much. I don't even have to play at all, if we don't want to leave the Copper Country. I know it's a shock that it came so soon, but we've talked about having more."

She pulled her head away from Darío and said, "I know, but not so soon. I can't—" She suddenly stopped, and both Charlie and Darío looked to the door to see if someone had come in. But no, it was Katie's thoughts that had stopped dead in their tracks. "Oh my God, I can't believe I'm going to have another baby." Her voice cracked and the squished-up look of disbelief was gone, replaced with a bright smile, lighting up her gorgeous face.

"Do you know how long I wanted a baby?" she said to Charlie who just held his hands up in a questioning motion. He was a guy. He knew to just stay quiet when a woman asked a question like that. She wasn't really looking for an answer. "And now, to have two babies." She looked away from Charlie and to her husband.

Darío had always seemed like a cool customer to Charlie, usually showing very little emotion, certainly never falling into the Latin hothead stereotype. But the guy was now a total pile of mush as he looked at his wife and slowly placed his hand on her still-flat stomach.

Charlie was just about to give them the room when Lizzie Robbins came through the door from the great room. She stopped abruptly when she saw Darío and Katie's tender embrace, her eyes zooming to Darío's hand on Katie.

Charlie knew from Petey and Darío that Lizzie, Katie, and Alison had been friends since grade school, and you could sure see it now—the simple, almost telepathic way the women had of communicating.

Lizzie's eyes went wide. She looked pointedly at Katie. Katie gave just the tiniest of nods and placed her hand on top of Darío's. Lizzie brought her hand to her chest and whispered, "Oh, Kat," her eyes already filling with tears. Katie nodded again, her head bobbing wildly this time, her tears coming freely now as she smiled. Stepping away from Darío, Katie met Lizzie halfway, and they embraced. The tears continued even as both women pulled away, now laughing.

Darío and Charlie looked at each other and just shrugged, totally out of their element.

"Oh, Kat, this is so wonderful. Were you guys trying?"

"No. This is a complete shock." She turned and smiled at Darío. "A good shock. A wonderful shock." She reached a hand out to her husband while one hand still clutched Lizzie's. Darío stepped forward and took his wife's hand. "An *awesome* shock," she added quietly, looking at her husband, who softly smiled and nodded his agreement.

"Holy wah, are you going to have your hands full," Lizzie said. Charlie waited for the panic to cross Katie's face, but no, she only grinned and nodded, then started laughing.

"You betcha, eh," Katie said, in a deep Yooper accent. She let go of Lizzie's hand to wrap both her arms around her husband's neck. "And I couldn't be more happy. I am so blessed." She leaned in and kissed Darío, making Charlie both uncomfortable and envious.

"Get a room," Lizzie said, breezing past the couple and making her way to the beer. She seemed to notice Charlie for the first time, and he joined her at the counter, giving Katie and Darío some space as the couple continued to gaze at each other, kiss, nuzzle, and just generally be mushy.

"How've you been, Charlie?" Lizzie asked him as she pulled two bottles of beer out, wiped them off on the towel next to the sink and opened them up.

"I've been okay. How about—"

"Hey, you're single, right? Are you here alone?" Lizzie interrupted him.

"Umm…."

"You have to think about whether or not you're single?"

"No, it's just…." He thought about his night with Phee. And her stupid rule about no mundane details. He'd spent the last three weeks playing that over and over in his mind and was now sure that she'd never had any intention of seeing him again, that she'd done it to protect herself.

Which was fine, and he understood it. But, God, that night had been so honest, so real. And now he wondered if it wasn't all a lie on her part.

"Yes, I'm single," he said to Lizzie. "And here alone." He

put a teasing tone in his voice as he continued, "But I thought you were happily married, Lizzie."

She swatted him on the arm. "Oh, you're just the cutest thing, Charlie Simpson." She took a drink of beer and studied him. After a second, she handed him the other beer. "I'm here with Finn's sister. She's a tiny blonde wearing a gorgeous red dress. Find her and bring her this for me. Her name is Phoebe."

He raised a brow at her, and she smiled. "Do it. You can thank me in your wedding toast." He laughed, and then his throat caught just a little bit as he remembered all the thoughts that had run through his head in the hours between leaving Phee at the diner and returning Saturday night to find her gone. Yes, he had to admit, even random thoughts of marriage had crossed his mind during that great day.

All to be shattered later that night.

He started to hand the bottle of beer back to Lizzie. "You know what? I don't think I'm in the best mood—"

Lizzie pushed the bottle back at him. "Red dress. Can't miss her. Do it."

Man, he could see how she made a living telling professional athletes and politicians how to run their lives. He gave in, said "Congratulations" to the still hugging and kissing Katie and Darío as he passed them, and exited the kitchen into the great room.

He scanned the room looking for a tiny blonde in a red dress and his mind went back to the tiny blonde he wished were in the room. God, Phee would look incredible in a red dress. Maybe a little strapless number that would caress those hot curves.

But nobody in the room matched Lizzie's description of her sister-in-law, and Charlie moved to the other side of the room, leaning against the built-in bookcases that surrounded the huge stone fireplace.

He'd been here a couple of times during the renovation when Petey had wanted his feedback, but he hadn't been back since the flooring and paint had been done, and certainly not with all the furnishings and accessories in. The great room was a *great* room—earth tones complementing the stone fireplace, splashes of color here and there. It looked like they'd rearranged the furniture a bit for the party, clearing out a spot right in front of the huge window that overlooked the lake. The huge Christmas tree stood in the middle of that area, and boughs of holly framed the fireplace. The furniture was pushed back and curved around, leaving a spot open, almost like someone was going to sing later or something.

Charlie wouldn't put it past Petey to fly in some hotshot pop star to perform at his holiday as a surprise to his guests, and possibly even to Alison.

There didn't seem to be any evidence of a band or piano or anything, though. The stereo system was behind Charlie, and he made his way over to it, placing the beer for the blonde on one of shelves next to it. Holiday music was currently playing on someone's iPod in the docking station, but several CDs were scattered on top of the receiver as well, as if waiting their turn. One in particular caught Charlie's eye, and he opened the case and put the CD in the player. When he had it set to the right track, he cut the iPod and switched the audio to the CD.

The beginning horn section of Al Green's "Let's Stay

Together" sounded, and Charlie took a swig of his beer, remembering the last time he'd heard the song.

Chapter Six

The Friday night after Thanksgiving.

A nd number five? That would have to be *Top Gun*."

"Seriously? *Top Gun* is in your top five? Over *Princess Bride*? Over *Citizen Kane*?" Phee asked him.

Charlie shrugged. "I didn't judge yours. *Sense and Sensibility*? Seriously?" he said, mimicking her tone.

She giggled. "Come on. It's a classic."

"But not nearly as cool as *Top Gun*."

Their hands were tangled, had been in some form of contact since folding the napkins nearly two hours earlier. Except for when Phee had crossed to the jukebox and put what must have been twenty quarters in, since they'd had soft standards playing for them while they'd talked. And talked. And talked some more.

Charlie couldn't ever remember being so at ease, so comfortable.

"Oh, I love this song," Phee said as "Let's Stay Together" came on.

"Me too," Charlie said. "Gotta be in my top five of all time songs."

"Songs. That's one we didn't do," Phee said.

Though he had loved the evening they shared, Charlie didn't want to talk anymore. And he didn't want to just hold her hand. He slid from his seat, not breaking his hold, and tugged on her hand as he stood. "Dance with me," he said.

"Here?"

He nodded. "Why not?" He tugged again, and she followed. He led her to the middle of the floor, out of view from the one window where the blinds weren't drawn. He pulled her into his arms, holding her right hand, her left resting on his shoulder.

It felt so right, so natural to be dancing with this woman. It seemed unreal that he'd only met her hours ago. They fit.

"This is nice," she murmured, and stepped even closer to him, her breasts grazing his chest.

"Mmm-hmm," he mumbled, sliding his hand up her back as Al Green sang about never being untrue.

She looked up at him. "Does it seem weird that we just met?"

"Yes and no," he said honestly. She nodded, getting it, and then placed her head on his chest.

They swayed together, hands slowly exploring, her head burrowing into his shoulder. All too soon the short song came to an end, and Charlie silently prayed the next song would be a slow one so he wouldn't have to let this girl go.

Ever.

The intensity of his thoughts—his feelings—should have scared him, but it didn't. They stood tentatively in that moment between songs, not wanting to break apart. And then the music started, and it was "Let's Stay Together" again. Phee's head sprang up from his chest, surprise in her pretty brown eyes.

"You didn't play it twice?" he asked, but already knew the answer.

"No," she whispered.

Her mouth looked so soft, so sweet, and Charlie knew he had to taste her. He lowered his head slowly, giving her time to turn away, but she didn't. No, the sweet, lovely girl in his arms rose up slightly and met him halfway. Her lips were warm and as soft as they'd looked. She tasted of coffee, deep and rich.

She opened to him right away, and he swept his tongue into her mouth, hers happily meeting him. Her arms wrapped around his neck, his around her back.

"Charlie," she whispered as he broke the kiss to move to her neck. His name had never sounded so sweet.

Nibbling up and down her neck, he heard himself groan. His hands roamed down her back, trying to touch every inch of her, wanting to remember her—this night— forever. Slowly, his hands moved down to her ass. That shapely, enticing ass which had mesmerized him from the first moment he saw her walking away.

He should stop. He had just met this girl, and he was pawing her all over. He was the nice guy, every girl's buddy, someone who'd never made a move on the girl he was supposedly crazy about.

And suddenly, with crystal clarity, Charlie saw the difference in what he'd felt for Deni and this burning, aching need he felt for Phee. Even after only knowing Phee for so short a time.

This was not the sweet, good-natured feelings he had with Deni that he had thought would grow deeper. This was already deep, deeper than he'd felt about a woman before.

A panic went through him about leaving town, leaving Phee, after this weekend. The urgency played out in his touch, his grasp of her little curvy body, as he slid his hands lower, needing to feel the skin of her legs. Praying she wasn't wearing hose or any other kind of barrier.

She wasn't. Her legs were blessedly bare under the skirt of her uniform. A skirt he hurriedly slid up and over that delectable butt, feeling the silk of her panties. But even that was too much of a barrier. His hands started to pull at the offending scrap of material, but Phee pulled away from him.

"Charlie," she said, breathing heavily, making him realize he was, too. He was just about to apologize, to tell her he'd stop, when she added, "Not here." She looked around wildly, then took his hand and led him past the jukebox—their song now winding down for a second time —and through the closest door, which was to the men's room.

"Phee, I...." But he didn't know what to say to this little blond sprite who had awakened him to feelings he hadn't thought possible.

"Shhh," she said, placing a finger against his lips. She backed up, still leading him with her other hand. She stopped when she ran into the vanity behind her. Her hand left his and she reached down and slipped her fingers just inside his belt, tugging him toward her.

He bumped into her, pushing her against the sink counter. Phee moved her hand behind her back as she untied her apron and placed it on the counter beside her, the change from her tips in the apron pocket jangling against the laminate countertop, some of the coins rolling out and onto the floor.

"Leave 'em," she said when Charlie made to retrieve them. "This is more important," she said, taking his face in her hands. "Isn't it?" she asked softly, looking up at him.

She wasn't asking him if sex was more important than the quarters still rolling around the floor. She was asking for something much more, and Charlie had absolute certainty in his answer. "Yes. More important," he said and she smiled. She started to kiss him again, but he added, "*Most* important."

She got it, and whispered, "Me, too."

Her hands trembled a little as she reached for the hem of Charlie's sweater, and he noticed his were trembling too as he started to unbutton her uniform. Only to find the buttons were fake, decorative only, and that he was not able to peel the polyester disaster from her to touch, taste and gaze upon her pale skin.

"Zipper's in the back," Phee said, then kissed him with a growing passion that matched his own. "Get this thing off me," she added, though Charlie was already unzipping.

Her skin was so soft, and he ran his hands up her arms after peeling the uniform down her body. He felt her kick the thing away from around her feet. He hated to break away from the kiss, but he needed to feel her against his bare chest. Regretfully leaving her lush mouth, he made quick work of his knit tee, then quickly returned to kissing her.

Holy shit! Her body pressed against his might have been the best thing he'd ever felt. Curvy and warm and soft. She smelled of vanilla and just a bit of…bacon? Which made him even harder.

His senses were whirling. He needed to see her. Stepping back, he broke their kiss and looked at her. Just… looked at her.

She stood before him in sensible white cotton bra and panties. "I wasn't expecting to be showing my underwear tonight," she said, embarrassment in her voice.

"You're beautiful," he said, meaning every word. A small blush crept up her chest, to her neck, and then to that adorable face.

She hopped up onto the counter. Charlie reached to help her, but she was already perched and reaching for him. He stepped between her open legs, his hands resting on her waist. She began to unbutton and then to unzip his jeans. Her small, warm hand reached into his boxers and grasped his hard-on. "Jesus, Phee," he hissed, then bent to kiss her again.

He couldn't get enough of her. Her mouth. Her full breasts, which he now held, squeezed, and teased with his hands. He pulled the cups of her bra down, not even bothering to unsnap it, needing his mouth on her too badly.

"Charlie," she moaned as he sucked a hard nipple into his mouth. Her foot ran up his thigh, her knees spreading wider to give him better access. She pushed his jeans and boxers down over his hips, freeing his cock. She grasped him once again and started slowly stroking.

He continued feasting on her breasts, moving to the other one while trying to keep his cool so he didn't come too soon. He wanted this to last.

But then she twisted away from him, her hand leaving his erection. "What?" he said, gasping for air.

"Just…this…." she said, reaching for her apron.

"What?" he said. The blood had left his brain, and he couldn't think beyond getting his mouth back on her and his cock buried deep inside her.

She pulled some quarters out of the pocket. Apparently not all of them littered the floor. She handed them to him and then pointed to the wall. And a condom dispenser.

Charlie chuckled as he fed the quarters into the machine. "Classy place you work in."

She laughed. "Don't I know it. But really, are you complaining?"

He took the packet from the dispenser and ripped it open. She took it from his hands and rolled it on him. She rocked back and forth, helping him as he peeled her panties off. He stepped in between her spread legs once again. Taking her face in his hands, he looked at her and asked quietly, "You sure?"

She swallowed, licked her lips, and nodded. "Very," she said as she guided him to her.

"Holy wah," she whispered as he pushed into her. A fleeting feeling of familiarity at hearing those words rushed through Charlie's head, but then she clenched around him and he didn't—*couldn't*—think about anything other than making love to Phee.

Chapter Seven

Three weeks later

The strains of "Let's Stay Together" wafted upstairs to Phoebe where she sat in the guest room that Alison had assigned to her earlier when she'd dressed for the party.

God, she'd played that night over in her head so many times in the past three weeks, but hearing that song gave her a physical pang of emptiness. And horniness.

She'd never had a one-night stand before. In fairness, she hadn't really thought it would only be one night while Charlie held her in his arms. And it might not have been if she hadn't received the call about Clea. She'd never know.

"Oh, there you are. I sent a good-looking young man to bring you a beer, did he find you?"

Phoebe shook her head. "No. I came up here for a minute to…to…." She looked around desperately, trying to think of a reason that she needed to escape the party.

"To have a moment to yourself?" Lizzie diplomatically offered.

"Yes, exactly. They're great people, and I want to thank you for bringing me, making me get out of the house."

"But whatever has been bothering you isn't going to go away by a cute boy bringing you beer."

Phoebe smiled. "Because he's not the *right* boy."

"Understood." Lizzie joined her where she sat on the edge of bed. "Are you sure you want to leave Port Huron?"

"It doesn't matter. He's not there anymore anyway."

"Where is he?"

Phoebe's voice caught as she tried to speak, and she finally just held her hands up in a "who knows" fashion. "Oh, honey," Lizzie said, putting an arm around her.

She told Lizzie the story, or most of it. She mentioned the instant chemistry she'd felt with a guy she met in the diner, how they talked all night and had made a bone-deep connection. She didn't tell Lizzie she'd had sex on the bathroom counter, but judging by Lizzie's blush, Phoebe figured her sister-in-law got the point.

"And I blew it. I totally blew it. I thought I was protecting myself in case he didn't show up the next night. No risk, right? He shows up, we spill all our personal info, then become damn Facebook friends or something. Or, he doesn't show, and I don't get all obsessive about him, because I can't." She felt something wet on her cheeks and realized they were falling tears.

Lizzie squeezed her even tighter, but waited for Phoebe to go on. "And then the next day...."

"Finn called about Clea," Lizzie finished for her. "Oh, Phoebe, I'm so sorry. There's no way Finn—or Clea for that matter—would have wanted you to drop everything and come home. Especially if they had any idea what being at the diner that night meant to you."

"I know. But I wanted to come home for Gran. It was important to me."

Lizzie nodded, stroking Phoebe's bare shoulder. "Pheebs," she said quietly, "why didn't you just wait and come home the next day?"

It was the question Phoebe had asked herself every day in the past three weeks. She knew the answer. She just hadn't admitted it, even to herself. "I was scared," she said.

"Wasn't Finn clear that Clea wasn't in immediate danger? I told him to make that very clear. I knew I should have talked to—"

"That wasn't it. I mean, I was concerned about Gran, of course, but Finn was clear about her condition." Lizzie waited. Phoebe took a deep breath, running her hands across her face and wiping away her tears. "What I felt for this guy was so real it scared me. When we left the diner, I hoped he'd come back the next night, but like I said, I'd protected myself if he didn't. But all that morning, I started thinking about if he did. I mean, really thinking about it. Beyond, 'Oh, he likes me.'"

She clasped her hands in her lap, her skin even paler than normal against the red satin of Alison's dress. "It was real, Lizzie. And deep. Even though we'd only met, it was like…we knew. You know?"

Lizzie nodded. "Sometimes you just know."

"And I knew. And I also knew this was it. No more roommates and loser boyfriends that I could walk away from, or who could walk away from me. This was grown-up time."

"That is some scary shit, for sure," Lizzie said.

"And I know I want what you and Finn have. But, if I'm being honest, I think on some level I picked loser boyfriends because I knew there was no risk of a future together. That I wasn't ready, or because of my messed-up mom, I didn't deserve it or something."

"Of course you deserve happiness. With a good guy." Lizzie emphasized the last.

"I know that…in theory."

"But in reality?"

She shrugged, unable to escape the truth. "In reality, when it became a possibility, I took the first chance I could to run like hell."

"Well, you know…."

"But I came to my senses. Right around Marquette, I pulled over and called the diner to ask the owner to pass on my cell number if a guy came looking for me."

"See. Your good sense overrode your fear. Good girl."

"Yeah, except I'd already quit with no notice. The owner laughed and told me to…you know. He wasn't going to be helping me out anytime soon."

"But you had made the choice to follow through, right? To try for a grown-up, real relationship with this guy?" Phoebe nodded her head, and Lizzie continued. "That's so huge, Pheebs. That's, like, ninety percent of the battle."

She shrugged. "Maybe, but the realization came too late."

"Bah-humbug. Don't be a Scrooge, even if 'tis the season."

"Huh?"

Lizzie was already standing up and pacing in front of Phoebe. "First thing tomorrow we'll make a list. We'll deconstruct that night minute by minute." At Phoebe's look of shock, Lizzie laughed. "Well, not *those* minutes. But all the stuff you guys talked about. I know you said you didn't do the contact info stuff, but I'll bet we can get some clues." She was talking to herself now. "The *right* clues. And then we'll get online. This is going to be a cinch."

"Wow," Phoebe said. Lizzie stopped her plotting and looked at her. "Finn didn't stand a chance, did he?"

A beguiling smile crossed Lizzie's face. "Nope. Not a chance."

"And thank God for that," Phoebe said and rose from the bed to give Lizzie a hug.

"There you are," Alison said, entering the room with Katie Luna behind her. Phoebe had met Katie at the same time she'd met Alison, though Katie's breathtaking beauty had intimidated the crap out of Phoebe. She seemed really nice, though.

There was a pointed look between Lizzie and Katie, and Katie gave a small nod. "You told her?" Lizzie asked.

"Yes," Katie said. Both women moved into the room, joining hands, and then hugs, with Lizzie. Phoebe found herself right in the middle of the group hug.

"Katie's pregnant," Lizzie said as the women untangled themselves.

"Oh, congratulations," Phoebe said. "But. Don't you… didn't you…?" She was trying to remember the news that Lizzie kept her apprised of.

"Have a baby just last winter? Just ten months ago? Yes,

that was me," Katie said, a laugh gurgling up as she finished. "I know, I know. I'm going to have my hands full."

"You know what's so weird," Lizzie said. "I said to Phoebe on the drive over here that I thought we were going to hear some baby news tonight." She pointed at Alison. "I just thought it was going to come from you."

"Well…." Alison said.

"You're not?"

"No, not pregnant. But I do have some news."

Phoebe saw Lizzie and Katie shoot glances at Alison's very bare left ring finger.

Alison looked at her bare wrist, like there was a watch on it. "In about ten minutes, I'm going to become Mrs. Petey Ryan."

Phoebe felt like she was in a room of fifteen-year-old girls, not late-thirties women, based on the shrieks and whoops.

"Katie, will you be my matron of honor?" Alison asked after the hugging and giggling settled down.

Katie said yes, and the two women hugged. Then Katie looked from Alison to Lizzie and back again to Alison, her brow raised in question.

Phoebe felt Lizzie stiffen beside her. Lizzie had Alison and Katie as her co-maids of honor at her wedding. Phoebe thought she remembered Lizzie mentioning that she and Alison were co-maids for Katie.

Phoebe was about to put her arm around her obviously hurt sister-in-law when Alison said, "Don't worry, Lizard, you're involved, too."

"What, am I reading a scripture or some such bullshit?

You know, it's bad enough you didn't tell me so I could help you plan, but—"

"Zip it, Lizard. You're not reading a scripture," Alison said and then waited for what Phoebe took as dramatic effect. "You're Petey's best man."

Chapter Eight

⁂

Al must have just told the girls," Petey said, explaining the girlie shrieking and giggling coming from upstairs. "Lizzie is going to be pissed that she didn't get to plan this."

"Plan what? The party?" Charlie asked. He and Petey stood on the edge of the great room, near the hallway that led to the stairs in one direction and to the main entryway in the other.

"It's more than a party, Charlie. I'm about—Becks! You finally made it. I thought you two might be no-shows. And believe me, you wouldn't have wanted to miss this party."

Charlie turned to see Sawyer Beck and Deni Casparich walking toward them, hand in hand. Sawyer, like all the men present, had on a suit and tie. It was the first time Charlie had seen him so dressed up. And Deni….

"Wow," he said as the couple stopped in front of Charlie and Petey.

"Deni," Petey said. "Holy shit, you clean up good."

Not quite how Charlie would have put it, but it was certainly true. Her brown hair, usually in a ponytail, was down and curled loosely, and she was wearing a green dress that had a poofy skirt. And heels. Charlie didn't think he'd ever seen his buddy in heels before.

Deni took Petey's compliment in stride. "Thanks, Petey. You don't look so bad yourself."

In fact, Charlie had to admit, Petey looked the most… civilized that he'd ever seen the jock. Clean-shaven, hair recently cut, impeccable black suit with a silk tie, even a jaunty red pocket square.

"Well you know, host and all. Couldn't let any of the guests show me up," Petey said.

"No chance of that," Sawyer said. They both said hello to Charlie. Most of the awkwardness around the couple was gone now, but there was always just a hint of possessiveness on Sawyer's part whenever Charlie was around. Which was fine with Charlie. He suspected Deni secretly liked it.

He did miss his confidant, though. He would have liked to have told Deni all about Phee and have her pat his back with comfort. But those days were no more. And given how happy Deni had been these past nine months, Charlie could live with that.

"What took you guys so long, anyway?" Petey said.

Deni and Sawyer exchanged a look filled with intimacy and a knowing that Charlie now recognized. He'd shared a look like that with Phee while they'd danced—a silent agreement.

"Well, we had a little side trip on our way here," Deni said.

"Oh, details, details," Petey said.

No, no details, Charlie thought. He was over his crush on Deni, but he certainly didn't want to hear about their quickie on the way to the party.

"Not that kind of side trip," Deni said.

"Dude, get your mind out of the gutter," Sawyer said. "That's my fiancée you're talking about." A big grin filled Sawyer's face as Deni unlinked her hand from his and showed off a huge rock on her left ring finger.

"No shit? Man, that's great," Petey said, shaking Sawyer's hand. The big man then bent down to kiss Deni on the cheek. Charlie was waiting for some crack, but Petey merely said, "You've got a good man, Deni, but he's truly the lucky one."

"Awww, thanks, Petey," Deni said.

The happy couple looked at Charlie, then away. He took a step closer to them and stuck out his hand to Sawyer. "Congratulations. Really."

Sawyer shook Charlie's hand and nodded. Deni kissed Charlie on the cheek, looking at him with what was near pity. He took her hand, looked her in the eye, and said, "Really, Deni, I am *very* happy for you."

"Thanks, Charlie," she said softly, her smile returning.

"Sorry to steal your thunder, Becks," Petey said. "But I can top that, 'cause in about ten minutes, I'm going to be the happiest man in the room."

"Yeah?" Sawyer said, "Why's that?"

Petey looked at his watch. "We're moments away from Alison walking down those steps to 'Here Comes The Bride.'"

"Seriously?" Charlie, Deni, and Sawyer all said at the same time.

Petey grinned. "You betcha."

It wasn't a vision of white that came flying down the stairs, but blue, as Lizzie Robbins quickly descended, saw Petey, and launched herself at him. He caught her and twirled her around, her blue dress gliding out behind them. He set her down. She stepped away and then hugged the big man once again.

"I'm so…." Lizzie choked up on her words, and Petey put his arm around her.

"I know, Lizard, I know. Me too." He squeezed her shoulder, then let her go. "Now, are you ready to be my best man?"

Lizzie smiled and nodded, wiping tears away. Man, there was a lot of stuff bringing Lizzie Robbins to tears tonight, Charlie thought to himself. He wasn't sure how well she knew Deni and Sawyer, but their news would probably bring on the waterworks, too.

Then, just as suddenly as they started, Lizzie's tears stopped. She jumped into action, walking deeper into the great room. "Okay, can I have everyone's attention? We need to get some people seated up front here, and…." Lizzie kept on with the instructions, but Charlie decided to head the other way. As he turned to move down the hallway, he saw a flash of a red dress at the top of the stairs, but the person hadn't moved down far enough for Charlie to see her face.

Probably the blonde in the red dress he was supposed to bring a beer to. He almost waited until she came fully into sight, but then he heard Lizzie announcing to all the guests what was about to happen and the cheers and buzz made him turn away.

He moved into the kitchen, in theory to get another beer, but in reality to take a break from all the happy news.

He'd meant what he'd said to Deni. He *was* happy for her and Sawyer. And Petey and Alison. And Katie and Darío with their baby news. But good God, how much love and joy was a broken-hearted fool supposed to bear?

He grabbed a beer out of the bucket and reached for a towel to wipe it down. Except it wasn't a towel. It was an apron tossed on the counter next to the sink.

And Charlie plummeted back into that glorious, cursed night with Phee.

Chapter Nine

❧

The Friday night after Thanksgiving

I don't want this night to end," Charlie said as he zipped up her uniform for her. He placed a soft kiss on her neck and ran his hands down her arms, squeezing her hands.

"I have news for you. The night has already ended." She took a quick glance at her watch, reluctant to take her hand from him, even for that second. "Maureen and Stan will be here in a half hour to prep for the breakfast shift. They're the owners."

"There can't possibly be anything left to prep. You've done, like, everything that could possibly be done to this place. They'll praise you for your diligence. You might even get a raise." His hands were on her waist now and stayed there as she turned to face him. She smiled at his words—knowing there would be no praise, and certainly no raise, from her stingy bosses. He smiled back at her, and her tummy did a little flip-flop. Or maybe it was her heart.

She wrapped her hands around his neck, pressing herself against his warm, hard body. She kissed him, softly at first, then deeper. His hands moved from her waist up her back, pulling her even closer. Then one hand slid down and cupped her butt. Against her tummy she felt the beginnings of another erection.

"No, really, we need to get out of here. Buddy's cool, but Stan and Maureen won't be pleased to know I spent the night here. And certainly not that I had sex in the bathroom."

She made quick work of cleaning the bathroom counter, slapping Charlie's hands away good-naturedly as he tried to remove her uniform once again. Admitting defeat, he handed her apron to her, which she quickly tied around her waist.

After she was satisfied with the bathroom, she led him out, holding his hand. She took him through the diner, stopping at his booth—*their booth*—to pull his coat from the hook. They walked on past the jukebox which now stood silent, their paid songs having run out at some point while Charlie had been deep inside her. They moved beyond the counter, and through the doors to the back. At the end of the kitchen was an alcove where each waitress had a locker holding her personal items and coat and such. She opened hers and started to bend over to get her boots.

"Here, let me," Charlie said as he knelt in front of her and gently lifted her foot up and slid her Nike off. It was the one concession to the retro uniforms that Stan and

Maureen would allow. After years of wearing spiky, high-heeled sandals as a cocktail waitress at the casino, Phoebe was giddy with relief to finally be able to wear comfortable shoes during a shift.

Charlie lifted her other foot and did the same. He took her boots from the floor of the locker and set them next to her feet. He then started to place the Nikes in her locker, but noticed the puddle of water that melted snow from her boots had created. Instead, he stood the shoes up, balancing them against the wall of the locker, so that they wouldn't get wet from the melted snow puddle.

The small, thoughtful gesture made Phoebe's throat close with emotion. She put a hand on Charlie's shoulder, in theory to balance herself, but in truth to feel him again. It had only been moments ago since he'd held her in his arms, and already she missed him.

Sliding the boots onto her feet, he looked up at her, and she knew he was feeling the same tumult of emotions that she was. When he finally stood, he skimmed his hands up her sides. Then he reached inside the locker and pulled out her scarf, which he gently wrapped around her neck. A neck he'd kissed and nuzzled and marked as his own. He helped her on with her coat and did up the toggle buttons for her. She then took his coat, which she'd swung over the locker door, and bundled him in it.

"Time to go," she said. Damn, if she started tearing up, she'd just die.

Charlie had a look of frustration on his face. "How do I see you again? You wouldn't even let us do last names. Mine is—"

She put a hand over his mouth, stopping him. "I know what I said. And I still stand by it. Even after we...even after." Giving him a warning look, she slowly took her hand away. "I'm here tonight. I start at four. I'm on until midnight." She took a deep breath, scared to do this and yet determined. "I really want to see you again, Charlie. But, after taking the day to think about it, if you only want it to have been one lovely night, I want to be okay with that." He started to interrupt her, but she held her hand up like she'd muzzle him again, and he stopped. "And it will be easier for me to be okay with it if I don't know anything more about you. Trust me on this."

"At least give me your last name," he said, with pleading in his voice.

"Just come back tomorrow. Tonight, I mean. I'll tell you then. I'll tell you every way to contact me that you want, but only tonight. And only because you want it to be for more than one night."

"That's crazy. What if something happens?"

That's what she was afraid of—something happening. But not the kind of thing he was thinking of. She was thinking that he'd change his mind and not show, and then Phoebe would be armed with too much information. She'd been a bit...aggressive in the past with boys who blew her off—following them on Facebook, hanging out in places she knew they'd be. But she'd worked past it, and for the first time in her life she didn't feel like she needed a man in her life to be complete.

And then Charlie had walked into her diner and rocked her world.

This guy is different. She knew it deep in her soul. And as warm and tingly as it made her feel, it also scared her a little. "If something happens, then it wasn't meant to be." Way more Zen than she actually felt, and yet she did feel that there was some cosmic serendipity at play here, had been the entire night, for her to feel so strongly so quickly.

"No. I can't...." He didn't finish his sentence, seeing the resolve on her face. He knew her well, even after such a short time.

"Tonight. I'll see you tonight," she said and kissed him goodbye.

$$\approx$$

Three weeks later

Charlie left the kitchen, but instead of heading back toward the great room, he made his way down the hallway to the entrance, stopping at the little alcove room that held all the outerwear. He reached for his boots, wanting to make his escape before the wedding ceremony began. He was happy for his friend, but all the memories of Phee that had been wafting around him all night had finally caught up with him, and he had to leave. The apron had been the last straw.

His boots stood in a pile of melted snow, and he flashed to his memory of standing Phee's tennis shoes out of the puddle at the bottom of her locker so they wouldn't get wet.

God, why did everything seem to remind him of her and that beautiful, magical, way-too-short night?

He'd been devastated the next evening when he'd gone

to the diner only to find that she'd quit her job with no notice and left town. Or so they'd said. The owners of the diner refused to give him any other information about her, not even her last name.

He supposed he didn't blame them. How were they supposed to know what had transpired the night before? And he wasn't about to tell them he'd had mind-blowing sex in their bathroom. He'd asked for Buddy, to corroborate his story that he was a friend of Phee's and meant no harm. But Buddy hadn't been working that night, or the next morning when Charlie had stopped again on his way out of town.

He stepped into the little room where everybody had thrown their coats and dug around for his. Stepping back into the hallway, his backside collided with someone. So, somebody else was ducking out from the happy nuptials. He turned at the same time that the person behind him did, coming face to face with her.

A vision in a strapless red dress. A tiny blonde. Lizzie's sister-in-law.

Phee.

"Phee?" He said, shocked. "How? Where?" He raised his hands to take hold of her arms but stopped, as if touching her might break whatever spell had conjured her presence.

She stood staring at him, her mouth open in shock.

She must have recovered before he did, because she blurted out at a rapid pace, "My name is Phoebe Lynn Robbins. I'm staying with my brother, Finn, and his wife at the family farm on Paradise Road. That's in Houghton. I went to Houghton High School. I shared an apartment in Port Huron, but I'm not going back anyway, so you don't need that address." She took a quick, deep breath and continued on, "I'm on Facebook as Phoebe Robbins. I'm on Twitter as at PheebsYooper, but I'm hardly ever on that. My Gmail account is Phoebe Robbins twenty-seven, no spaces. My cell number is—"

"Phee, stop," he said, this time taking hold of her arms like he wanted. God, she *was* real. And warm. And soft. And blathering on about stupid stuff.

Stuff like—oh. "That's right. No way for you not to find me now, Charlie."

"Oh, I won't need to find you again," he said. She looked up at him, hurt in her eyes. He ran his hands down her arms to clasp her hands in his. "Because I'm not going to let you go again."

"Oh, Charlie," she whispered. Then she smiled, and his insides melted faster than the snow on his boots.

"I'm Charlie Simpson, by the way. I live here and work at Summers and Beck."

"You live here? In the Copper Country? I...I can't believe it."

It had seemed like some kind of Christmas miracle that they'd found each other at all that first night, but then to find each other again....

"Amazing," they both said, then smiled.

"Hey, you two," someone said from behind Phee. "Look up." They did to find they were standing under a sprig of mistletoe.

They smiled at each other. From the other room, Charlie heard a deep voice declare, "Dearly beloved...." Then he heard nothing but Phee's gasp as he took her in his arms and kissed her.

"Merry Christmas," he murmured against her lips, then kissed her again.

She kissed him back, twining her arms around his neck and melting into him. When they finally parted, she looked at him and said exactly what he was thinking, "Best Christmas gift ever."

Epilogue

❧❧❧

etey looked at the group gathered around Alison and him. His friends, his family, even Al's parents on a rare outing from the nursing home where they lived. They sat ensconced in comfortable chairs at the front of the area Al had created for their wedding.

There was only one person missing. He was glad he'd broken Al's rule and told Zeke Hampton about the wedding. Zeke had wanted to come, but was currently on cruise with the Navy. Honestly, though, Lizzie was as appropriate to be Petey's best man as Zeke.

He looked down at his sweet, ballsy Al, a vision in white. Not really a bridal dress, because that wasn't her style. In fact, he was kind of shocked she'd even bowed to the convention of wearing white. It was kind of like the famous Marilyn Monroe dress, full skirt with a halter neckline. At least that's what he'd heard her call it. He knew jack shit about necklines.

She was a vision, though, that was for sure. He just

couldn't believe that she'd finally said yes to his proposals. But that was how he'd been so successful in the NHL— brow-beating and tearing down the other guys so that by the third period, anytime they saw him coming, they just got out of his way.

It was kind of like that with Al. By the time she saw him go down on one knee—*again*—she'd just sighed and said yes.

The minister droned on. Christ, how long did it take to make his girl legally his, anyway? And everybody there had better realize that they were going to get their asses kicked out about twenty minutes after Al and he said "I do." He was all for having a celebratory toast, but then he wanted to hustle his bride—*bride! Holy wah!*—up the stairs and into their newly posh master suite.

Out of the corner of his eye, he saw Charlie come into the living room from the hallway. Petey hadn't even realized his new buddy wasn't in the room. Petey did a double take when he saw that the woman coming into the room with Charlie was Finn's little sister, Phoebe. And they were holding hands.

Well, that was fast. And yet, there seemed to be a familiarity that they displayed with each other. They stared into each other's eyes, Charlie slipped his arm around Phoebe's waist and she snuggled into his side, her arm wrapping around his waist.

Petey knew without a shadow of a doubt that in some crazy way, this was the girl who had Charlie moping about since Thanksgiving when he'd gone home. Petey tried to rack his brain as to where Finn's sister lived. He knew it was downstate somewhere, but he'd thought it was Detroit. But now, he'd bet on Port Huron.

The couple stood behind everyone else, and thus not seen by anyone but Petey and Alison. They looked at each other with dopey grins on their faces, and Petey instantly knew that his friend and Finn's sister had somehow found each other. And that they felt how he felt about his soon-to-be *(come on, already, padre!)* wife.

Deeply, hopelessly, forever in love.

Also By Mara Jacobs

Contemporary Romance ~ The Worth Series

Worth The Weight

Worth The Drive

Worth The Fall

Worth The Effort

Totally Worth Christmas

Worth The Price

Worth The Lies

Worth The Flight

Contemporary Romance ~ The Freshman Roommates Series

In Too Deep

In Too Fast

In Too Hard

Mystery ~ Anna Dawson's Vegas Series

Against The Odds

Against The Spread

Against The Rules

Against The Wall

Contemporary Romance

Instant Replay

Romantic Suspense

Broken Wings

Anthology

Countdown To A Kiss

Mara Jacobs is the New York Times and USA Today bestselling author of the Worth series.

After graduating from Michigan State University with a degree in advertising, Mara spent several years working at daily newspapers in advertising sales and production. This certainly prepared her for the world of deadlines!

She writes mysteries with romance, thrillers with romance, and romances with…well, you get it.

Forever a Yooper (someone who hails from Michigan's glorious Upper Peninsula), Mara now splits her time between the U.P. and Las Vegas.

Mara loves to hear from readers, contact her at:
www.marajacobs.com
mara@marajacobs.com

www.ingramcontent.com/pod-product-compliance
Lightning Source LLC
Chambersburg PA
CBHW020551130626
46552CB00007B/2861